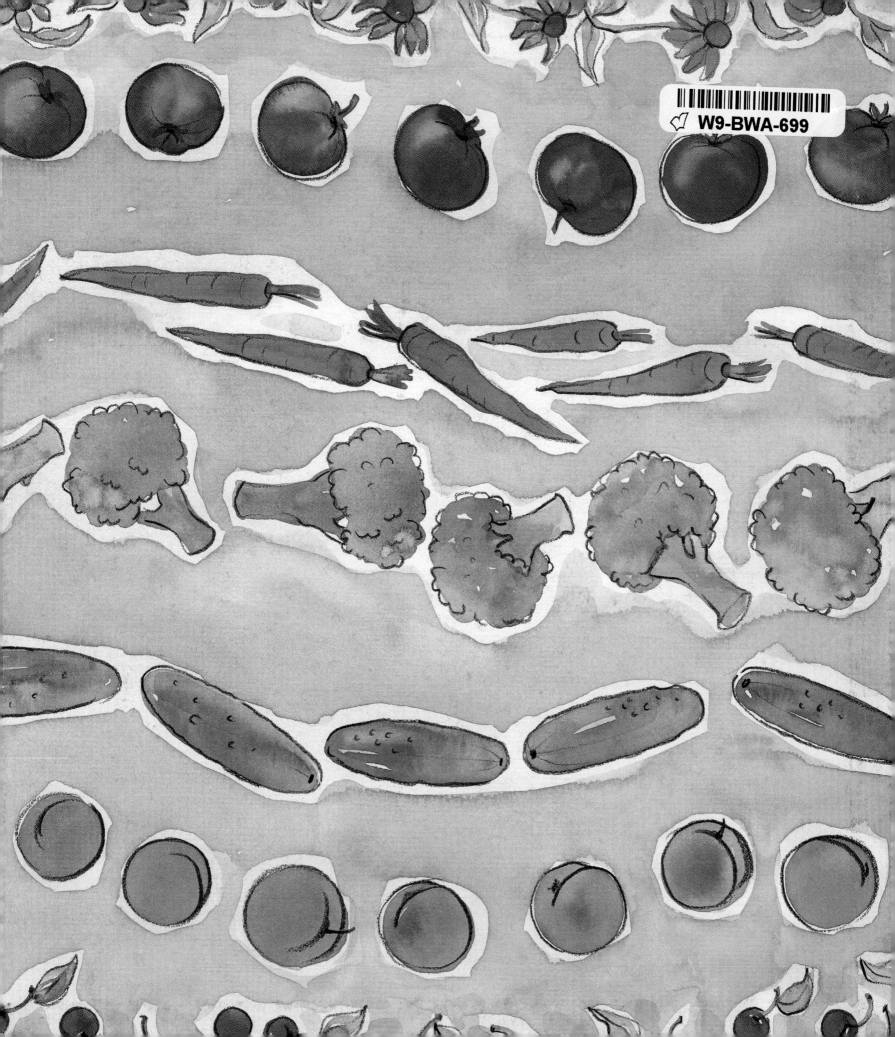

To my spirited trio, Michelle,
Terra, and Ana — S.T.

For my sweet girl, Bryn — J.D.

tiger tales
an imprint of ME Media, LLC
5 River Road, Suite 128, Wilton, CT 06897
Published in the United States 2013
Text copyright © 2013 Shanda Trent
Illustrations copyright © 2013 Jane Dippold
CIP data is available
ISBN-13: 978-1-58925-115-1
ISBN-10: 1-58925-115-6
Printed in China
TT/1400/0006/1012
All rights reserved
3 5 7 9 10 8 6 4 2

For more insight and activities,
visit us at www.tigertalesbooks.com

3/$5

99¢

FARMERS' MARKET DAY

TODAY'S SPECIAL

by

Shanda Trent

TODAY'S SPECIAL

Illustrated by

Jane Dippold

tiger tales

Hey! Wake up!
It's Saturday!
We can't be late
for Market Day!

I shake my piggy. Clink, clink, clink.
What will I buy? Hmm . . . let me think.

Our wagon bumps along the aisles.
Vegetables and fruit for miles.

99¢

A forest—green with broccoli trees,

99¢

50¢

cucumbers, and pods of peas.

$3

Bushels brim with fruit to eat:
Tomatoes, plums, and peaches—sweet.

50¢

75¢

Juicy cherries in a bunch,
Let's buy a basketful to munch.

Sweet and minty herbs and spices.

Mama stops to check the prices.

Flowers! Yellow, blue, and red.

A rainbow for our flowerbed.

Some kittens rub against my knees.
I want one, but they make Dad sneeze.

Blocks of beeswax, jars of honey.

Beeswax $2.00

Chewy, sticky,
sweet, and runny.

A bird feeder,
a house for bats,

Canvas bags,
and floppy hats.

Up above me, wind chimes dangle,
Singing out a jingle jangle.

$3

$6

I've finally found my prize . . .

I'll fill it at the kitchen sink
And give our thirsty plants a drink.

My legs are tired. I need a ride.
I move our stuff and climb inside.

I love
Farmers' Market Day.

$3

85¢

Let's bring a friend next Saturday!

$7

75¢

apples

99¢

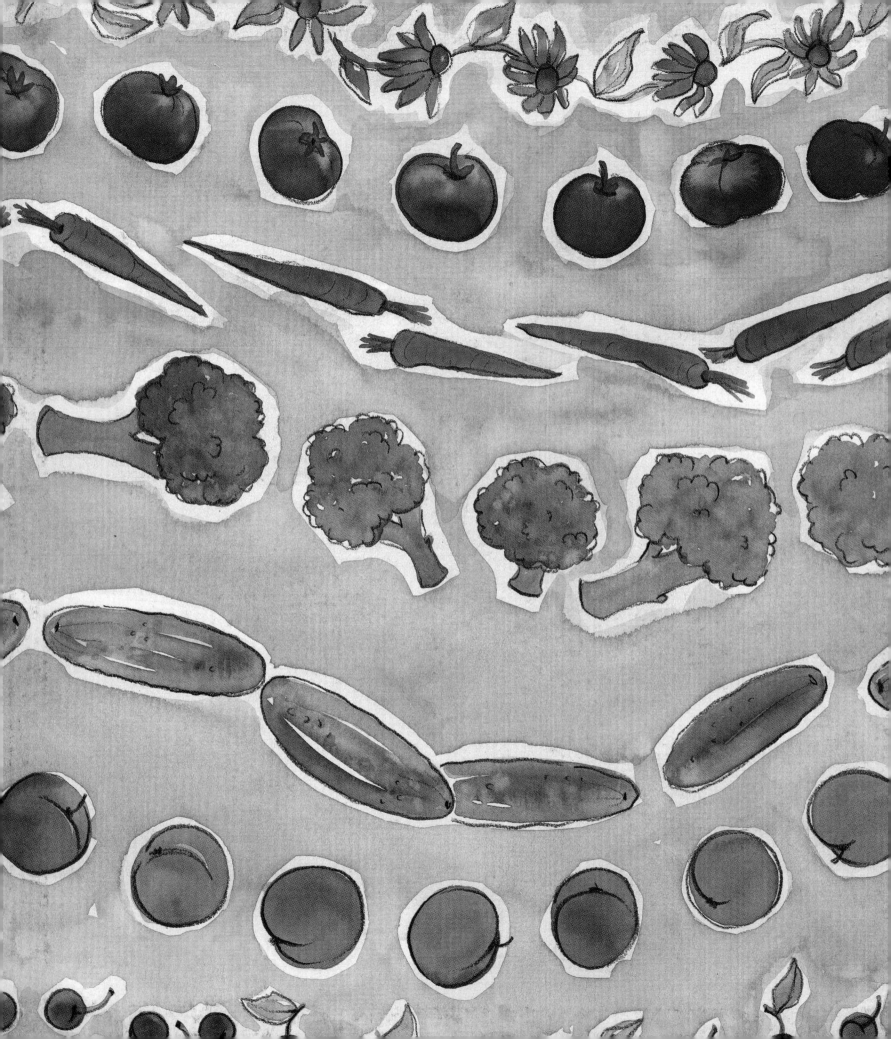